KT-491-541

Shona,
WORD
DETECTIVE

Shona, WORD DETECTIVE

John Agard

With illustrations by
Michael Broad

Barrington Stoke

For Father Stanley Maxwell

Maxy to us boys of Saint Stanislaus College, Georgetown, Guyana

A teacher who made the dictionary an adventure

First published in 2018 in Great Britain by
Barrington Stoke Ltd
18 Walker Street, Edinburgh, EH3 7LP

www.barringtonstoke.co.uk

Text © 2018 John Agard
Illustrations © 2018 Michael Broad

A CIP catalogue record for this book is available from the British Library upon request

ISBN: 978-1-78112-786-5

Printed in China by Leo

Contents

1   To be a maverick   1

2   Parrots speak a
dead language   7

3   Our own little
language-nest   10

4   You're all word-detectives   15

5   You still haven't told us
the name, Granny   23

6   Did the French really pinch
our roast beef?   28

7   Can't wait, can't wait   37

8   Bamboozled, betwattled
and bumbazed   46

Chapter 1

To be a maverick

Shona loved words. For as long as she could remember, Shona had written down strange words in a special little notebook.

One night, Shona's mum and dad were watching the news on the telly. Granny was having her usual doze in her rocking chair. Shona was curled up with a book on the sofa. She perked up her ears when the news reader said something about languages dying.

"... *According to the latest report from UNESCO, by the end of the 21st century some 600 languages will have become extinct ...*"

Shona knew the Dodo was sadly already extinct. But she'd never imagined a language could become extinct like that odd bird that is no more.

On the screen appeared a photo of a wise-looking man with feathers in his hair and a tattoo on his chin. The news reader said the man was an Elder of the Maori people and the last speaker of his native language. Then there was a comment from a woman, who looked very sunburned under her straw hat. Shona spotted 'LOL' written in big bold letters across her T-shirt.

"LOL?" Granny asked, as she jumped out of her snooze. "What on earth is LOL?"

"Laugh Out Loud," Shona said. "Teen talk, Granny. You know ... like text talk."

But this time Shona hadn't got it quite right. The 'LOL' on the woman's T-shirt meant *Language Our Lifeline*.

The LOL woman stared at the camera and spoke with a fire in her eyes. "With every bone in this body," she said, "I'll fight to help protect dying languages before I myself pass on ... or pop my clogs ... whichever you prefer. Mind you, I have no plans to push daisies or catch Charon's ferry just yet ..."

Shona started to giggle.

"What's so funny?" Shona's dad asked.

Well, to Shona's ears it sounded funny when the woman said she hadn't planned to *catch Charon's ferry just yet*. She made it sound as if she was catching a ferry across the English Channel. But Shona knew Charon was the guy who took the dead in his ferry across the River Styx. She had learned this from her book on Greek myths.

The news reader said that the 'LOL' woman was Professor Divina Crystal-Bloomer, known in certain circles as the 'maverick lexicographer'.

"She must be from Maverick," Shona said. She had heard of Limerick in Ireland but never of a place called Maverick.

Her mum laughed and explained, "It's not a town. People who think outside the box are often called 'maverick'."

"Like your Miss Bates, Shona," her dad added with that dry laugh of his. "The winner of last year's *Teacher of the Year Award!*"

"You're right, Dad," Shona said. "*Think outside the box.* That's what Miss Bates always says."

And that night Shona went to bed with one thought buzzing in her head. To be a maverick when she grew up.

Chapter 2

Parrots speak a dead language

When Shona googled the name 'Professor Divina Crystal-Bloomer', she discovered that the Prof had written a book called *If Parrots Can Be Bi-Lingual, So Can You.*

Professor Crystal-Bloomer said she'd been inspired by Alexander Von Humboldt, the 18th-century German explorer. When travelling up the Amazon river, Alexander had met his first electric eel. But the explorer had never in his wildest dreams expected to meet parrots that spoke a dead language.

Shona read that the reason for this oddity was that one tribe had been massacred by a rival tribe. With no one left of the first tribe, their language was left in the beaks of the parrots.

That's why Professor Crystal-Bloomer wanted to teach parrots languages that might soon be extinct. That way the parrots might save some of the sounds of a language that would otherwise be for ever lost when the last speaker died.

Chapter 3

Our own little language-nest

The next day at school, Shona told Miss Bates about Professor Divina Crystal-Bloomer. Miss Bates smiled like she was sharing a secret with herself.

"Oh, I've been to Divina's public talks," Miss Bates told her class. "Even got her to sign her book for me. She's known as the maverick lexicographer."

"What's a lexicographer, Miss?" someone asked.

"A person who compiles a lexicon ..." Miss Bates said.

"What's a lexicon, Miss?" someone else said.

"Oh, a lexicon is just another word for dictionary," Miss Bates said. "Professor Crystal-Bloomer is a lexicographer, which means she travels round the world compiling dictionaries. And she likes to find strange and beautiful words from dying languages ..."

'That's exactly what I'd like to be,' Shona thought. 'A *lexicographer ... a maverick* one like Professor Crystal-Bloomer. Then I'll travel the world saving words from going the way of the Dodo ...'

The voice of Miss Bates returned Shona from her day dreams. "Think of a lexicographer as a sort of word-detective ..."

"You mean like Sherlock Holmes?" a boy at the back said.

"Don't see why not," Miss Bates said. "But instead of looking for clues to solve the puzzle of a crime, you're looking for clues to solve the puzzle of a word ..."

Miss Bates held up a book. She was full of surprises like that. The book was her treasured copy of *If Parrots Can Be Bi-Lingual, So Can You*! It was signed by Professor Divina Crystal-Bloomer herself.

"This is the book that introduced me to the idea of a language-nest," Miss Bates said.

But the class hadn't a clue what Miss Bates was on about.

Language-nest?

'A nest has to do with birds, so could Miss Bates be talking about Professor Crystal-Bloomer's parrots?' Shona thought.

But no, it wasn't that. Miss Bates explained that the idea of a language-nest started in New Zealand as a way to save languages at risk of becoming extinct.

"A language-nest," she said, "is a nice way to bring together speakers of a language that's dying out. It's been used among the Aboriginal peoples of Australia. It's like a friendly time when the Elders gather together. They get the chance to natter in their own language and enjoy hearing others speak it too ..."

Shona's best friend, Ewa Wozniacka, was smiling because her first language was Polish. Ewa often told people that her surname was the same as Caroline Wozniacki, the tennis player born in Denmark who had Polish parents.

"Don't you worry, Ewa," Miss Bates said with a smile of her own. "You'll be able to show off your Polish soon when we transform this classroom into our own little language-nest. Watch this space!"

Chapter 4

You're all word-detectives

Shona couldn't wait to hear more about Miss Bates's plans for their own language-nest.

"Can we have a language-tree as well, Miss?" she asked. "Then the language-nest will have branches to sit on."

"Brilliant, Shona, you must be a mind-reader!" Miss Bates said, and clapped her hands. "First we'll transform that back wall into a big language-tree. With a lick of green paint and a bit of brown fabric for the trunk that wall will soon be in full bloom. But here comes the exciting part. For our *World Languages Day* celebration, we'll invite family and friends to get together for tea and cake and the chance to speak their own languages. Who knows, we might even have a sing-a-long in different languages ... right here in our language-nest."

Then Miss Bates told the class to think of themselves as word-detectives. Their job was to investigate the clues hidden right under their noses.

"Begin by looking around your homes ..." Miss Bates said. "Maybe there's an object with a name that has an interesting history ... Or something in a picture – the name of a tree, a river, a mountain, all these have their own story to tell. Ask yourself about the story behind the name of a person or a place. Look at old photos in your family album, and you might find a strange word from a journey to another continent. Ask your parents and grandparents about the pictures – another great way to involve them in our language-nest. Now, hands up all those who speak a language other than English ..."

Miss Bates nodded at Victor Alvarado whose arm had shot up.

"Spanish, Miss," Victor said. His mum and dad had named him after Victor Jara, as he told anyone who asked.

Victor Jara was a folk singer and songwriter from Chile. Sometimes Victor wouldn't say any more than that. Other times he'd repeat what he'd heard his parents say – "Victor Jara sang the truth for the hearts of the people of Chile, but he was murdered by the cruel people at the top who didn't like the words he sang."

The girl sitting next to Victor Alvarado then said, "I speak Akan."

She was Thema Ofosu. Her parents were from Ghana. Sometimes her friends would make a mistake and call her Thelma instead of Thema. They'd even shorten her name to 'T' and say, "*See ya, later, T ... Cool trainers, T ...*"

Thema preferred to be called Thema because her name means *Queen* in the Akan language.

"I'll speak Punjabi if you like, Miss ..." Kyle Singh said.

"Don't you worry, Kyle," Miss Bates said. "You'll get the chance to show off your Punjabi."

Kyle always wore his hair in a bright *patka* – today his *patka* was sky blue. Kyle loved to look like the cricketer Monty Panesar spinning for England in his trademark *patka*.

"And I speak Mandarin," one voice chirped up.

"And I speak Mandarin," said another voice, like an echo.

These voices belonged to the identical twins, Liang and Peng. Liang had told the class her name meant *graceful willow*. It made Shona think of a weeping willow, but Liang was always smiling and as graceful as her name.

Peng's name meant *giant bird*, but she didn't look like one to Shona. And just when Shona had thought she'd sussed out which twin was Liang, then Peng would smile and say, "No, I'm Peng ..."

Then a sudden outburst erupted at the back of the class!

"I can say hello in Italian. *CIAO* ..."

"I can say hello in Hebrew. *SHALOM* ..."

"I can say hello in Hindi. *NAMASTE* ..."

"I can say hello in Turkish. *MERHABA* ..."

20

"I can say hello in Japanese. *KON'NICHIWA ...*"

The outburst finished with Jack Hornsby's, "I can say hello in Aussie. *G'DAY, MATE.*"

Jack Hornsby's name always made Shona think of *Little Jack Horner sat in the corner.*

Jack's dad was English, and his mum was Australian. Jack was a bit of a joker who called his English friends *pommies*. And, just to wind them up, he'd break into Aussie talk they couldn't understand. Like he was doing right now with his *G'day, mate.*

"Please don't speak all at once!" Miss Bates said, but she was smiling at Jack's nonsense. "Goodness me! You lot will take some beating. I doubt Professor Crystal-Bloomer's parrots make half as much din as you do. Remember, now," Miss Bates went on, "you're all word-detectives, so good luck with your detecting."

Chapter 5

You still haven't told us the name, Granny

When Shona's parents saw her going round with a magnifying glass to one eye, they decided that Shona was going through a Sherlock Holmes phase.

There she was, rooting around in the kitchen, in the garden and in the shed. Then a brainwave told her to look in the attic, the same attic where Miss Bates had discovered a roost of *flittermice* with her bat-detector.

Flittermouse is how Germans describe bats, and Shona thought it made a bat sound so cute.

Shona was looking in her dad's clutter – sorry, *memorabilia* – when she came across an odd baskety thing. It was covered with a pile of old carpet tiles, but while the material felt like a basket, the shape wasn't right. It was long, like a tube.

Shona showed her mum the strange object.

"Where on earth did you get that?" her mum asked.

"Found it in the attic," Shona said. "But don't ask me what you're meant to do with it ..."

"I believe it comes from the Amerindians, but I can't remember the name. Ask your dad, he might remember ..."

Her dad turned away from the news. The way he examined the object up and down, you'd think he was an expert on the *Antiques Roadshow*.

"Man, the name is on the tip of my tongue," Shona's dad said. "But I can't for the life of me remember. Ahh, it's so annoying when that happens! Ask your grandmother ..."

"Don't know the last day me see one of these, me tell yuh," Granny said. She held the object as if it was a boa constrictor. "Brings back memories of when I worked a couple years as a midwife in the Guyana rainforest. Had my fair share of travelling by canoe down some big-big rivers. And you know how I can't swim. But by a wing and a prayer ... a wing and prayer saw me stay safe and sound."

"But you still haven't told us the name, Granny," Shona reminded her.

"*Matapi*," Granny said. "Pull it, man. The thing not a snake – won't bite you. See see for yourself how stretchy it will get. Flexible, very flexible. That's why the Amerindians use it for straining the poison-juice out of cassava, then they grate the cassava to make flour for their cassava bread ..."

"What's the name again, Granny?" Shona asked.

"M-A-T-A-P-I," Granny said, spelling out the word for Shona.

"Thanks, Granny." Shona grinned. "You've given me a great idea for my language-nest."

"Language-nest?" Granny repeated to herself. "This girl Shona like she's in a world of her own."

Chapter 6

Did the French really pinch our roast beef?

First, Shona wrote down the word *Matapi* in her little notebook in neat letters.

Shona called it *Shona's Thesaurus*. To be honest, she'd pinched the idea from *Roget's Thesaurus*, which was a book she often dipped into on her hunt for words.

Shona had learned that the word *thesaurus* came from the Greek word for *treasury*. And her notebook was full of her treasures!

'Ah, that's it ...' she'd thought to herself, '*Shona's Thesaurus* will do just fine.'

Just then, while her mum and dad watched telly, Shona heard some new news. Something about a new Far Right political party called the LLTB. Apparently LLTB stood for the *Less Languages the Better.*

Shona guessed they must be called Far Right because it sounded like their ideas were far from right. And when the LLTB leader's face appeared on the screen, he didn't make much sense to Shona. He had on serious spectacles, which made it look like he knew what he was talking about, but Shona didn't think he did.

"Now don't take this the wrong way," the LLTB leader said. "I'm all for everyone living together like one happy family. Call it a multi-culture, call it a rainbow nation, call it whatever you like. The name doesn't bother me. I'll tell you what bothers me ... the simple fact that there are far too many languages in the world. About 7,000 at the last count. The country of Papua New Guinea alone has over 850 languages. This can only lead to confusion and conflict ... I say we'd have a more peaceful world without so many languages getting in the way. Wouldn't a world in which everybody spoke the same language make life so much easier? And that's the message of the LLTB. Plain and simple. The less languages, the better ..."

As the leader of the LLTB rambled on, even the news reader, Jeremiah Makepeace, was at a loss for words. Shona could tell that Jeremiah Makepeace also thought the leader was talking rubbish, but he was doing his best to keep his face calm as he listened.

"So what do you think of the latest UNESCO report that over 200 languages are in danger of extinction?" Jeremiah Makepeace asked the LLTB leader.

"Now, Jeremiah, you know as well as I do that we're not talking about endangered animals here," the leader said. "It's only language, after all. You're making it sound like extinction is a dirty word. We all have to die one day ... even you, Jeremiah." The LLTB leader chuckled at his own joke.

"Don't you think speakers of a dying language might find your views upsetting ... even offensive?" Jeremiah asked in his no-nonsense way.

"I expect they will, Jeremiah, I expect they will ... but let's be honest ... wouldn't life be so much easier if everybody in the world just spoke one language? Think of the money saved on interpreters. As for those films with English sub-titles ... sometimes the words are so small, you can't read them. All that would be a thing of the past. Let's say you're in the Amazon, or in the middle of Afghanistan, wouldn't it be nice to sit back with the locals and carry on a civilised chat in English? It's about time we took back control of our English language."

Jeremiah squinted in disbelief for a moment, then asked the next question. "What if the Chinese said life would be easier if we all spoke Mandarin? After all, Mandarin is the world's most spoken language with close to one billion speakers."

"That just goes to prove my point, Jeremiah," the leader said. "If those one billion Mandarin speakers – I trust you counted them all – if they were brought up to speak English, then our French neighbours over the Channel wouldn't steal *our* words. Didn't the French pinch our roast beef and call it *le Rosbif*? Now if that isn't bare-faced theft, then you tell me what is, Jeremiah? Any fool can see that putting *le* in front of a word doesn't stop it being *our* roast beef!"

"There you've got your facts in a bit of muddle," Jeremiah said, as calm as a cucumber. "You'll find the word *Rosbif* came over the Channel when the Normans conquered England. It's the Brits who stole *Rosbif* from the French and turned it to roast beef. True or false?" Jeremiah Makepeace smiled as leaned forward. "*Vrai ou faux?*"

"You're not taking me seriously, Jeremiah ..."

"But wouldn't it be a *serious* old world if we all spoke the same old Queen's English?" Jeremiah asked.

"You're missing the point, Jeremiah ..."

"Answer the question, true or false?" Jeremiah kept on. "*Vrai ou faux, Monsieur?*"

But Jeremiah got no answer to this question. Instead, with a twinkle in his eye, he got in one more question. "And so will you tuck yourself into bed tonight with one of those films with the very small sub-titles?"

"Is this LLTB fellow for real?" Shona's mum asked, as she shook her head.

"He may have a point," Shona's dad said.

Shona looked at him in shock – he didn't agree with the LLTB leader, did he?

Then her dad burst into his wicked laugh and added, "But many a point has been known to be pointless."

"And Jesus wept," Granny said with a sigh. "And Jesus wept." This was Granny's favourite comment whenever she felt the world couldn't get any more confusing.

Shona didn't know what to make of it all either.

Chapter 7

Can't wait, can't wait

"So what have we got here, Shona?" Miss Bates asked when Shona turned up the next day with the long baskety object.

"Granny says it's a *matapi*," Shona said. "The Amerindians of the Caribbean use it to strain cassava."

"Ah, *matapi*, what a lovely word," Miss Bates said. "And what's our Ewa smiling about?"

"My *pisanka*, Miss," Ewa said. She pointed to a branch on the language-tree. "Looks like my *pisanka* has just been laid …"

Ewa had brought in a *pisanka*, which was a hard-boiled duck's egg her grandma had hand-painted with pretty swirls like a shell. Ewa's grandma – her *babka* – had told Ewa that in Poland they start to decorate the eggs on Ash Wednesday. That way they'd be nice and ready for Easter.

And there, glittering from another branch of the language-tree was Kyle's *maang tikka*.

"Sorry to disappoint you curry-lovers out there who were expecting *tikka masala*," Kyle declared, in his grown-up way of talking. He held up what looked like a necklace out of a fairy tale. "This here is my mum's *maang tikka* from when she got married. Trust me, it's very, very special. She showed me photos of her and Dad on their wedding day … Dad in his scarlet turban, Mum with her *maang tikka* round her forehead like she was Queen of the Punjab."

Kyle then broke into his best bhangra routine, dancing on one foot with his hands in the air, which sent the class into stitches.

"Poetry in motion," Miss Bates said, laughing. "Spoken like a true poet, Kyle. And your dance was the icing on the cake. Now let's see what you've got there, Thema Ofosu."

Thema put her finger to her lips, as if to keep them all in suspense. What was she hiding in that bag under her arm?

Like a magician pulling a rabbit from out of a hat, Thema produced the figure of a spiderman. She said that her grandad had carved it out of a coconut shell and sent it all the way from Ghana.

"Is that by any chance Anansi, the spiderman?" Miss Bates asked. "Up to his old tricks?"

Thema nodded, pleased that Miss Bates
knew of Anansi's cheeky tricks.

What Miss Bates didn't know was that *Anansi* meant *spider* in Thema's first language, Akan. And so, Thema hung Anansi on the language-tree, suspended in a web of white cotton. Close by was a beautiful instrument that Victor Alvarado had brought in.

"It looks like a sort of lute," Miss Bates said.

"It's a *charango*, Miss," Victor said. He plucked the strings and ran his hands along the smooth wood of the instrument. "The back of the *charango* comes from the shell of an armadillo," he told Miss Bates.

Then Miss Bates turned to the twins, Liang and Peng. "So what are you two hiding behind your backs?"

Without a word, Liang and Peng showed the class a pair of dolls dressed in silk robes. They said they were an Emperor and Empress from their grandmother's collection of Mandarin Opera puppet dolls.

"So how do you say doll in Mandarin?" Miss Bates asked.

The twins laughed and said with one voice, "*Doll.* Same as English."

"*Doll,*" Miss Bates repeated. "Did you hear that, class? The Mandarin for doll is *doll.* So we've been speaking Mandarin and didn't even know we were. Fabulous!" Miss Bates laughed.

Then she pointed to Jack Hornsby at the back of the class and rolled her eyes to the sky. "Dare I ask what Jack Hornsby is about to spring on us?"

And Jack Hornsby looked serious for once as he produced a *boomerang.* He said it had travelled a long way with his mum. A treasured gift from Celeste, a wise old Arrernte woman, when Jack's mum was a young girl in Australia.

LANGUAGE TREE

"And does the word *boomerang* have a special meaning?" Miss Bates asked.

"Don't know, Miss," Jack said. "Me mum reckons it's from an Aboriginal language that's gone extinct ..."

"All the more reason to have your *boomerang* on our language-tree for our *World Languages Day*," Miss Bates said.

The class erupted into a loud chorus of *"Can't wait, can't wait."*

Chapter 8

Bamboozled, betwattled and bumbazed

At last the day had arrived.

Outside their classroom hung a yellow banner you couldn't miss if you tried. Its bold black writing said –

This Way to Our Language-Nest!

The hall was filling up with mums, dads, grandmas, grandpas, aunts, uncles, friends and friends of friends.

You could feel the excitement in the air. And that wasn't just because of the blessing of the April sunshine, which had perked up people's strides and put a smile back on their faces.

Miss Bates flitted about in her spring blouse. She felt ever so pleased with the handiwork of her flock of word-detectives. She greeted people as they arrived and checked the microphone was working. *"Hello, hello! Testing one two three!"*

In short, Miss Bates was being an expert multi-tasker!

When everybody had settled down, Miss Bates said a few words of welcome.

Everyone knew that Miss Bates was full of surprises. But no one could have known the surprise that was to come.

Miss Bates paused and then declared, "And now I'd like to invite to the stage a special someone who kindly accepted my invite to our language-nest, despite her hectic life ... Someone who's come all the way from Papua New Guinea to be with us today ... Someone who needs no introduction ... So please put your hands together and make some noise for Professor Divina Crystal-Bloomer of *Language Our Lifeline* fame!"

Shona couldn't believe her ears – or her eyes – when the very woman she'd seen on the telly appeared from behind the curtains.

But there she stood in the flesh. For real.

It was Professor Divina Crystal-Bloomer – with a parrot perched on her shoulder like Long John Silver, the pirate from *Treasure Island*.

First, Professor Crystal-Bloomer apologised for her parrot. "Please excuse Polly Parrot if she comes out with anything rude," she said, and nodded at the parrot.

Needless to say, the very word *rude* grabbed the children by the ears.

Professor Crystal-Bloomer smiled. "Mind you," she said, "Polly can suffer from stage fright at big events like this. But don't be fooled. She's a proper little Amazonian diva, aren't you, Polly?"

"*Deeeeva deeeeva deeeeva!*" the parrot parroted back.

And the children giggled at how *rude* it was.

"So tell us, Polly – and don't go all shy on me – how you feeling in front of all these good people?"

It sounded to Shona like Professor Crystal-Bloomer was interviewing the parrot.

"*Bamboozled! ... betwattled! ... bumbazed!*" the parrot answered back.

The children put their hands to their lips in shock. Polly had just said a very rude word that began with B!

"Oh no, children, *bumbazed* isn't at all rude." The Professor winked at them as she went on. "The words *bamboozled*, *betwattled* and *bumbazed* all mean *to be confused*. And isn't it a shame such lovely word-gems have disappeared?"

"*QUAKEBOTTOM! QUAKEBOTTOM! QUAKEBOTTOM!*" Polly squawked.

"Sounds like Polly's being rude again, Miss," someone at the back shouted.

"Funny thing is, there's always someone who thinks our Polly is being rude," Professor Crystal-Bloomer said. "But Polly has just told you an extinct word that means a coward – a scaredy-cat. Quakebottoms not only shake with fear in their boots ... they quake with fear in their bottoms."

Truth be told, you probably shouldn't think about Professor Crystal-Bloomer's impression of a quaking bottom for too long.

Then the Professor asked all the men with a moustache to stand up.

"You, Sir," she said. "You too in the third row … you there with the green hat. How long did it take you gentlemen to grow your *grass belong mouth*?"

The dads, uncles and grandpas all looked a little *bamboozled*, *betwattled* and *bumbazed*.

Then the Professor told them that people from Papua New Guinea say *grass belong mouth* to mean a moustache.

"Such a charming expression," Professor Crystal-Bloomer said. "That's why we of LOL say *Language Our Lifeline*. What do we say?"

"*Language Our Lifeline*," the children parroted.

The Professor walked into the crowd with the microphone.

"Gimme an L ... gimme an O ... gimme an L ..." she said.

"L-O-L," the children belted out, only too happy to join in.

The Professor grinned as she got ready to pop the surprise of the day. "Now I will introduce a dear friend of mine," she declared. "We go back a long way ..."

And who should take to the stage, peering over his serious spectacles?

None other than the LLTB leader that Jeremiah Makepeace had interviewed on the telly.

"Isn't that the crazy LLTB man?" Shona's mum said. She nudged Shona's dad. "The one waffling on about less languages the better?"

"Mr Pointless in person, yes," Shona's dad said with a wink.

No one had a clue what was going on. But
Miss Bates was smiling to herself as if she
might be *in the know*.

It all became clear when Professor Crystal-Bloomer said that her friend in the spectacles was an actor. And for an April Fool trick, he'd agreed to act the part of the leader of the LLTB. The Less Languages the Better was a silly *made-up* political party.

Jeremiah Makepeace had been in on the trick. He'd agreed to play along in a pretend interview, because it was for a good cause.

The cause of making everyone aware of dying languages.

Shona knew then that she would never forget that day – the day their language-nest had brought together so many faces, old and young, and so many words. All sorts of words from all over the world.

Shona also knew she wouldn't forget Professor Crystal-Bloomer, the maverick lexicographer, and Polly, her amazing parrot.

And that very night, before she forgot, Shona went home and wrote down ...

betwattled

bamboozled

bumbazed

not to mention

Quakebottom ...

All in her little notebook. Her *Shona's Thesaurus*.

Our books are tested
for children and young people by
children and young people.

Thanks to everyone who consulted on
a manuscript for their time and effort in
helping us to make our books better
for our readers.